MW01434602

DISCARDED
Property of
Louisville Public Library

WHERE DO YOU HIDE TWO ELEPHANTS?

Written by Emily Rodda   Illustrated by Andrew McLean

Gareth Stevens Publishing
A WORLD ALMANAC EDUCATION GROUP COMPANY

I met two elephants today. They were in a hurry.
One of them was lean and mean, the other sad and sorry.

TUSK
LATES
CAFE
TUSKER
The Elegant Elephant
TRICKS
MASKS
COMICS
CARDS
GAMES
ELEPHANT
CORNER
MAGIC SHOP
CAFE TUSKE
HOT DOG

Lean-and-Mean roared, "Help us! Quick!"
Sad-and-Sorry cried, "Major Tooth is after us!
We need a place to hide! Major Tooth is nasty,
and cruel as cruel can be.

Hide us! Please! Or we'll be caught!"
So I said, "Follow me."

I found a clever hiding place.

7

But then as you can see ...

"Hide us! Quick!" the elephants said.
So I said, "Follow me."

I found another hiding place.

11

But then as you can see …

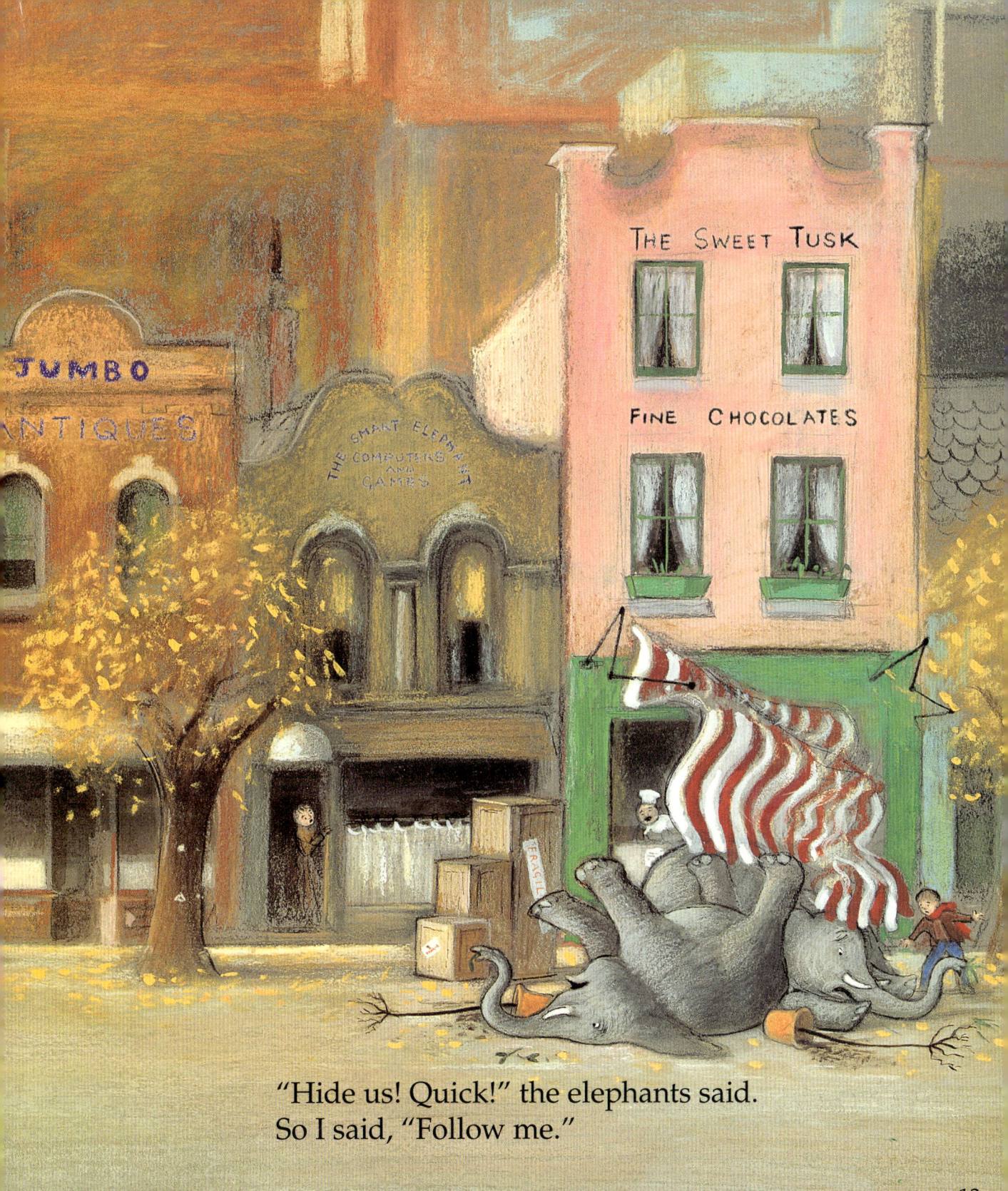

"Hide us! Quick!" the elephants said.
So I said, "Follow me."

I found another hiding place.

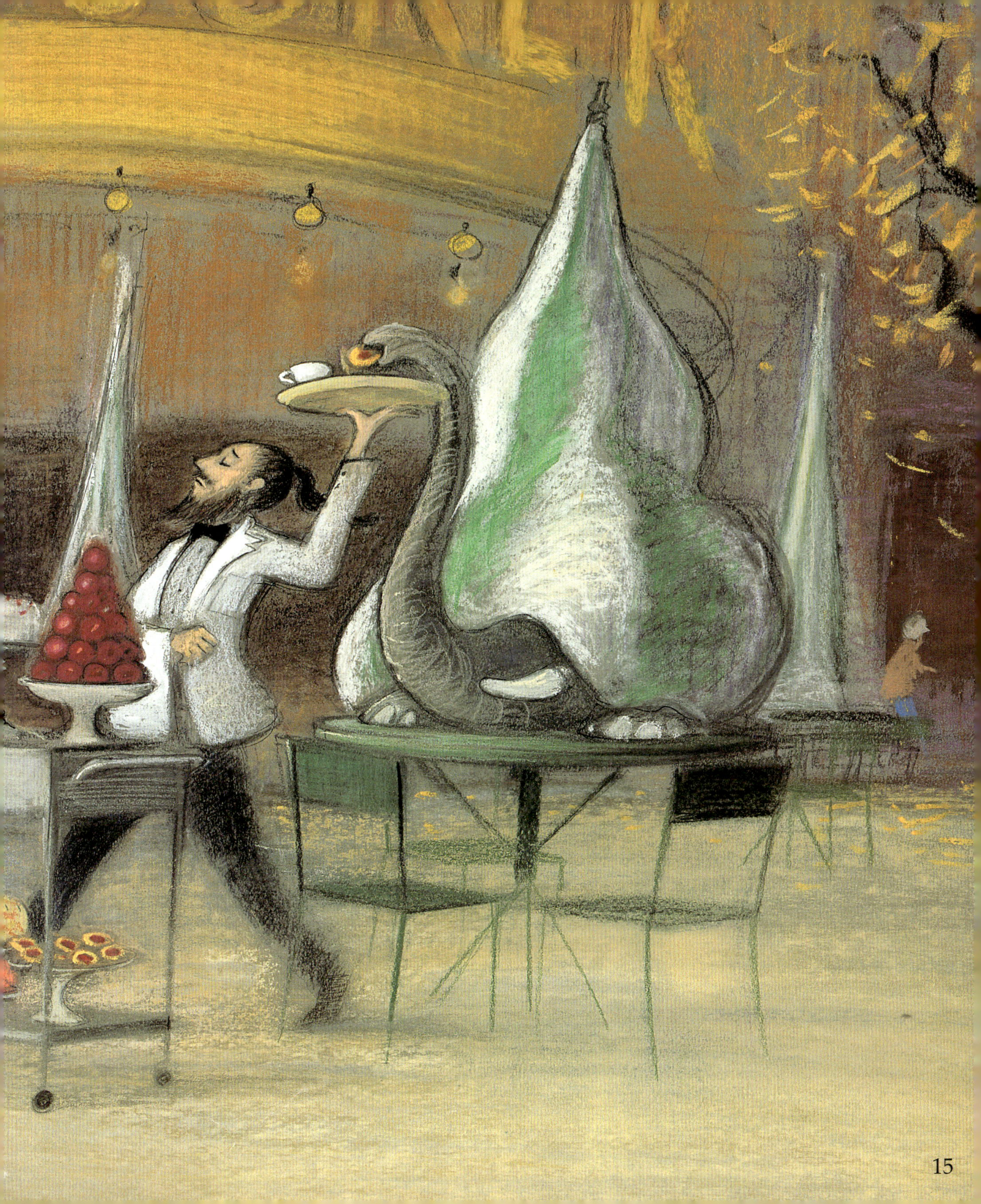

But then as you can see ...

"Hide us! Quick!" the elephants said.
So I said, "Follow me."

I found **another** hiding place.

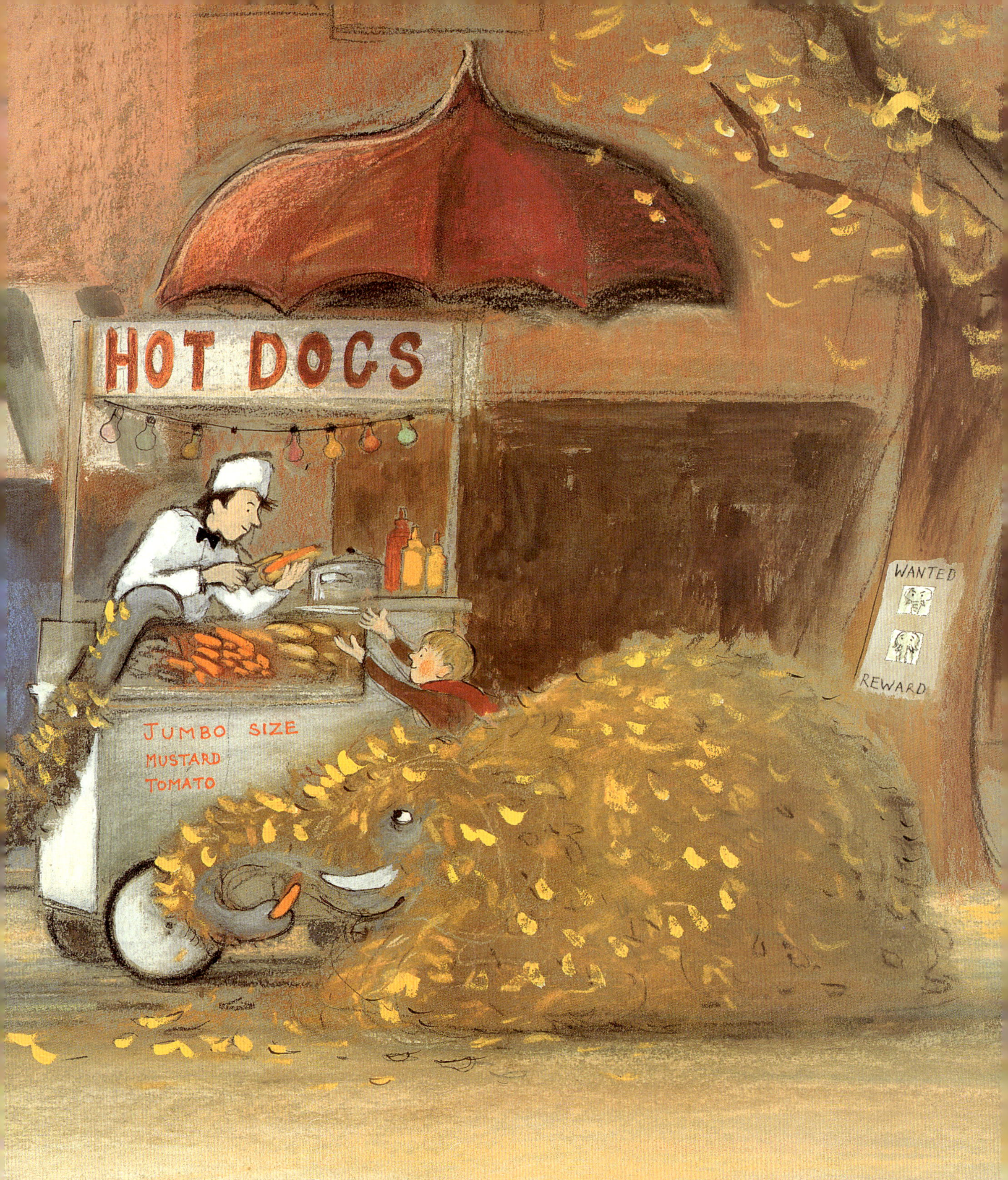
HOT DOGS
JUMBO SIZE
MUSTARD
TOMATO
WANTED
REWARD

But then as you can see …

"Hide us! Quick!" the elephants said.
So I said, "Follow me."

I found **another** hiding place.

23

But then as you can see ...
"Gotcha!" bellowed Major Tooth. "Now come along with me."

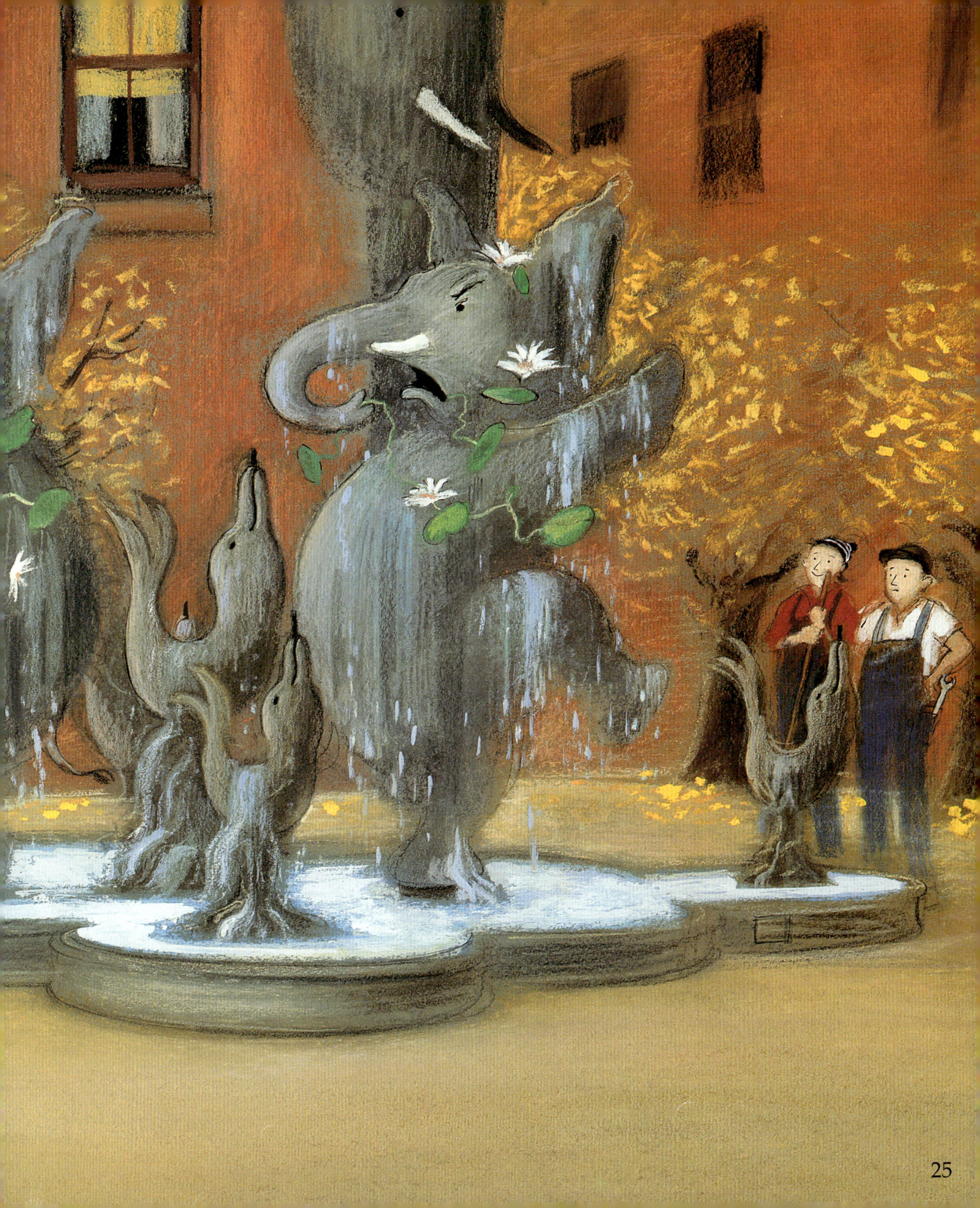

The policeman looked at Sad-and-Sorry. He looked at Lean-and-Mean.

"*These* aren't your beasties, sir," he said. "They're much too fat and clean."

27

"Oh, rats! You're right!" growled Major Tooth.
He raged and stamped his feet.
"On with the hunt!" the others yelled, and ran off down the street.

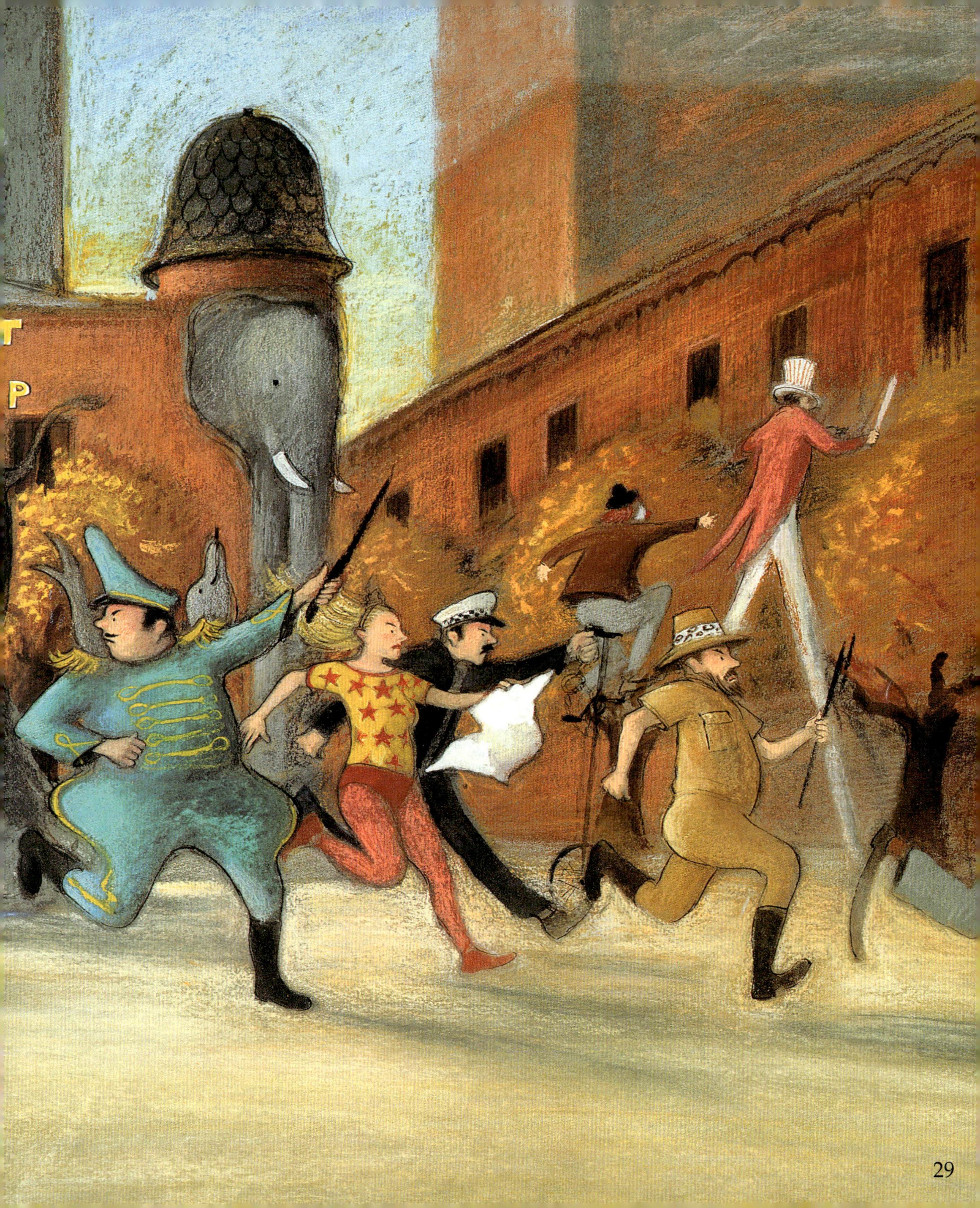

"Hooray! We're safe!" the elephants said. "How lovely to be free. But *now* we need a place to stay."

So they came home with me.

For Hugo Moline, friend of elephants – E. R.
For Alexandra, Angus and Catriona – A. McL.

Please visit our web site at: www.garethstevens.com
For a free color catalog describing Gareth Stevens'
list of high-quality books and multimedia programs,
call 1-800-542-2595 (USA) or 1-800-461-9120 (Canada).
Gareth Stevens Publishing's Fax: (414) 332-3567.

Library of Congress Cataloging-in-Publication Data

Rodda, Emily.
 Where do you hide two elephants? / written by Emily Rodda;
illustrated by Andrew McLean.
  p. cm.
 Summary: A boy finds a series of ingenious hiding places to save
two elephants from the nasty Major Tooth.
 ISBN 0-8368-2898-4 (lib. bdg.)
 [1. Elephants—Fiction.] I. McLean, Andrew, 1946- ill. II. Title.
PZ7.R5996Wh 2001
[E]—dc21   2001020161

This edition first published in 2001 by
Gareth Stevens Publishing
A World Almanac Education Group Company
330 West Olive Street, Suite 100
Milwaukee, WI 53212 USA

This edition © 2001 by Gareth Stevens, Inc. First published
in Australia by Working Title Press, Adelaide. Text © 1998
by Emily Rodda. Illustrations © 1998 by Andrew McLean.

All rights reserved. No part of this book may be reproduced,
stored in a retrieval system, or transmitted in any form or by
any means, electronic, mechanical, photocopying, recording,
or otherwise, without the prior written permission of the
copyright holder.

Printed in the United States of America

1 2 3 4 5 6 7 8 9 05 04 03 02 01

3 1397 00215 3883

AR SCHOOL COLLECTIONS
1.3 - ROD   c.2

Rodda, Emily

Where do you hide two elephants?

DISCARDED

AR 1.3   #53251   pts. 0.5

LOUISVILLE PUBLIC LIBRARY
Louisville, OH 44641

Fine on overdue books will be charged at the rate of five or ten cents per day. A borrower must pay for damage to a book and for replacing a lost book.